Jul. 7, 2010

ALGONQUIN AREA PUBLIC LIBRARY DISTRICT

10663289

SCRATCH
on the
PIRATE'S SHOULDER

For Michael, my own Captain Bligh.
Shiver my timbers!
And
For Fang and Fluffy, Felis and Hairylegs,
Tre, Tumnus and especially Gilbert.
Prrrrr—JG

For my wonderful family of Katz—
Mike, Rita, Che, Joel and Leah—MV

SCRATCH KITTEN
on the
PIRATE'S SHOULDER

JESSICA GREEN • MITCH VANE

LITTLE HARE
www.littleharebooks.com

Algonquin Area Public Library
2600 Harnish Drive
Algonquin, IL 60102

Little Hare Books
8/21 Mary Street, Surry Hills
NSW 2010 AUSTRALIA

www.littleharebooks.com

Text copyright © Jessica Green 2008
Illustrations copyright © Mitch Vane 2008

First published in 2008

All rights reserved. No part of this publication may be reproduced,
stored in a retrieval system or transmitted in any form or by any means,
electronic, mechanical, photocopying, recording or otherwise, without
the prior written permission of the publisher.

National Library of Australia
Cataloguing-in-Publication entry
Green, Jessica.
Scratch Kitten on the pirate's shoulder.

For primary school age.
ISBN 978 1 921272 45 5 (pbk.).

I. Vane, Mitch. II. Title.

A823.4

Cover design by Lore Foye
Set in 17/24 pt Bembo by Clinton Ellicott
Printed in China by Imago

5 4 3 2 1

Contents

How It All Began

Scratch and Peg-leg had been cast adrift because they'd put a mouse in the captain's stew. Now they were alone on the ocean in a tiny dinghy. The sun shone hot and no breeze blew. But now, at last, rescue was at hand.

Scratch teetered on the side of the boat as he watched a ship with black sails draw closer. He swished his tail. It was the closest thing he had to a flag.

'Shiver my whiskers,' he yowled. 'We're saved!'

Scratch was so excited he didn't notice the ship was a leaky, shabby old tub. He didn't care that its sails were black, or that the mainsail had a picture of a white skull wearing an eye patch.

But Peg-leg covered his eyes and screeched.

The ship drew alongside, towering above the dinghy like a shark over a fish. Men hung over the railing and shouted. A man with a long, tousled braid of hair threw down a rope.

It tangled around Peg-leg's feet so that he fell over. The sailors laughed, but Scratch wasted no time on Peg-leg. He leapt at the rope, clawed his way up it and jumped aboard.

1.
Rescued
by Pirates!

A fuzzy-haired man with a big red nose said they should leave Peg-leg in the dinghy. But the captain, who was a fearsome tall man, didn't agree.

'No, Fuzz,' he said. 'We might be able to sell him.'

So they hauled Peg-leg up onto the deck.

Scratch looked around. This ship
wasn't as shipshape and tidy as the
Silk'n'Spice had been. It had three
splintery masts. Piles of uncoiled ropes
lay in tangled heaps. The black sails
had patches and the woodwork had
not seen a paintbrush for many years.

At the prow a wooden figurehead
poked out over the water. Someone
had painted her dress pink and
seagulls roosted on her head.

The captain glared at Peg-leg.
He had a hooked nose and a great
tangle of black hair and beard.
A cutlass was tucked into his belt,
and a black patch covered one eye.
Peg-leg couldn't take his eyes off him,

but Scratch was more interested in the colourful parrot sitting on the captain's shoulder.

'I didn't do nothing!' whined Peg-leg. His voice shook with terror. 'I was set adrift for no reason. All I want to do is get home.'

The captain laughed. 'We can help you get home, all right! Find a job for him, Barnacle!'

A pirate whose face was bumpy with warts grabbed Peg-leg's arm. 'Aye,' he growled. 'He can *earn* his passage home or walk the plank!'

'And if he makes it home, we'll even hand him over,' said the captain. 'Perhaps alive! So long as someone pays us enough gold!'

'*Squawk*!' screamed the parrot. 'Give us a cold! Give us a cold!'

'*Gold*, not *cold*, you stupid bird!' the captain growled. The parrot tucked its head under its wing and then wriggled under the captain's beard.

Scratch wondered why the parrot would hide its head when it had such a good view of everything.

'Well, don't stand there like a pack of landlubbers!' shouted the captain. 'Flop-eye Fred and Toothless Terry, tie that dinghy's rope to the railing! Gappy, Stinky and Paddy, trim the sails! Unlucky Luke and Unluckier Larry, it's your turn to watch out fore-and-aft.'

The men rushed to obey orders.

'And don't you expect a free ride, cat!' roared the Captain, glaring at Scratch. 'You'd better prove *your* worth pretty fast or you'll be swimming home!'

Scratch flattened his ears and scurried to hide behind Peg-leg. But Barnacle was already dragging Peg-leg away.

'And you'd better round up some decent grub, Spew!' the captain bellowed at the cook.

'That's right, Spew!' Barnacle growled. 'If you give us weevil waffles again we'll eat *you*!'

Peg-leg turned to look over his shoulder. 'Ahem, Captain sir,' he said. 'I'm a ship's cook . . . one of the best!'

'Why didn't you say so?' cried the captain. 'Take him to the galley, Barnacle. Let's see what he's worth! If he's as good as he says, we'll keep him. But if he's as useless as Spew, he'll walk the plank!'

Peg-leg was dragged to the galley and Spew headed for the rigging. Cooking on board a pirate ship was dangerous if you couldn't cook. Spew was happy to let Peg-leg take the risk.

Scratch made a closer examination of the ship. It was filthy. He sniffed around the rope coils and stared in disgust at the mouse droppings which littered the deck.

'That bird is a lazy thing,' thought Scratch to himself. 'It sits on the captain's shoulder doing nothing while mice take over the ship!'

This gave Scratch an idea. If he and Peg-leg had to earn their passage home, Scratch would do what he did best. He would catch mice.

2.
Scratch Gets It Wrong

On the *Patch's Glory*, the galley was a
rickety wooden shelter on the
mid-deck. It wasn't the nicest place
to work, but Peg-leg did his best.
It was either that or walk the plank.

'Come and get it!' he croaked as he
dragged a pot onto the deck.

Men swarmed from all over the
ship to sit on the boards and eat.

For a while the only sounds were slurping, crunching, burps and grunts.

'Where did you learn to cook like this?' asked Fuzz.

'I've been a ship's cook for years,' Peg-leg boasted. 'I'm famous for my sardine pie and shellfish dip, not to mention my squid-in-the-hole!'

He was interrupted by a hoarse squeak. Spike, the cabin boy, was pointing a shaking finger at a small pile of mice by the deck rail. Scratch sat next to it, purring proudly.

'Captain Patch will kill us all!' Spike whispered.

'What have you done, cat!' Fuzz cried. 'Quick, Spike! Get rid of them!'

Spike, Fuzz and Flop-eye jumped to scoop up the mice and hurl them overboard. But they weren't quick enough. Captain Patch was coming to get his meal, and they had left a mouse on the deck. The captain almost trod on it.

'Oh, my skull and crossbones!' he roared. 'A dead mouse!'

He picked it up and
glared at Scratch.

'Is this your doing, cat?' he roared.
'No mouse is to be killed on
my ship! Don't you ever do this
again, or you'll take a walk on
the plank!'

'The stalk of a plant! *Awwk!*'
screeched the parrot.

Scratch slunk away to hide behind a bucket.

'It's not good for a pirate to be in love,' muttered Fuzz when the captain had gone back to his cabin. 'Everything reminds him of his sweetheart. Especially sweet little mice!'

'As for that deaf parrot!' said Ben. 'Just because Kate gave it to him, the captain says it can do no wrong.'

'It's about as useful as a chocolate teapot!' said Spike.

'Makes me ashamed to be a pirate,' growled Barnacle.

'We should cook it up in a parrot pie,' muttered Spew. 'But Captain Patch would feed us to the sharks if we harmed a feather on its head.'

'How interesting!' thought Scratch as he washed between his claws. 'The bird is useless, but it stays on board. I catch mice, but the captain wants me to walk the plank. This is a very strange ship.'

3.
Feathered Friends

When the parrot wasn't on the captain's shoulder, it lived in a cage on the foredeck. The cage was perched on top of a barrel in the shade, safe from sailors' feet. The door was left open so the parrot could come and go as it pleased.

That afternoon Captain Patch sat in his cabin counting his tiny pile of gold coins while the pirates played cards on the rear deck. Scratch decided to pay the bird a visit.

'I'm Scratch,' he told it. 'I'm a ship's cat.'

'I'm Squawk,' said the bird. 'I'm a pirate's parrot.'

Then the bird began to snuffle and squeak. 'Woe is me!' it whimpered. 'All I want is a peaceful life!'

Scratch pricked up his ears. 'Do you mean you don't like being a pirate's parrot?' he asked.

'Of course I don't,' squawked Squawk. 'Kate only gave me to the captain so he would remember her. Every time I shout in the captain's ear, it makes him think of her.

I've tried to be a good parrot,
Scraps. But it doesn't help. I still
don't like it!'

Scratch licked his forepaw to help
him think.

So the parrot's job was to sit on the
captain's shoulder and shout in
his ear? Scratch thought he could
do that as well as a parrot.

All he had to do was help the
parrot find another job.

'You know,' Scratch said at last,
'maybe Kate made a mistake. You
aren't really cut out to be a pirate's
parrot. Maybe you're really supposed
to be a . . . a *seagull*!'

He wondered if the parrot would
believe him.

'A ship's *hull*?' asked Squawk.

'No, a *seagull!* Look at them up there! They just fly around the masts and roost on the yardarms. It's a free, peaceful life.'

The parrot tilted his head and looked up. He saw the seagulls playing tag, chattering and having fun. None of them were sitting on a pirate's shoulder or shouting pirate things.

'I think you could be right,' he said.

Scratch purred. He didn't think it would be this easy to trick the bird! He hoped it would be just as easy to take the job on Captain Patch's shoulder.

Squawk hopped to the cage door. He shook his feathers and flapped his wings. Then he lurched clumsily forward, flew over the ship's rail and doubled back. Flapping as hard as he could, he circled the mast and then fluttered up through the rigging to the crow's nest.

'I'm a freegull!' he screeched.

Then he launched into the air
again and joined the mob of seagulls
that wheeled above the topmast.

'*Aarrk! Aarrk!*' the gulls screeched.

'Shaarrk! Shaarrk!' screeched
Squawk.

Scratch jumped down from the
barrel and set off in search of
Captain Patch.

The captain was on the bridge with Bad Benji and Flop-eye Fred.

'I say we go west,' Benji said.

Fred's glass eye flopped from side to side as he shook his head. 'We need to go east,' he growled.

Scratch jumped onto the helm.

'Silence, both of you!' growled Captain Patch. 'I'd rather listen to the bird than you two. Fetch it up here, Flop-eye!'

Fred hurried to do as he was ordered and Benji followed.

Suddenly Captain Patch noticed the scruffy kitten perched on the helm. 'Ain't you the one that killed a mouse?' he roared. 'I haven't forgotten that, you know.'

Scratch's legs told him to run away, but his mind told him to stay. He had to get the parrot's job, and now was his chance. With a brave mew, he jumped onto the pirate's shoulder.

Then he took a deep breath and yowled in his best pirate voice. '*Rrrowwwrrr!*'

Before he knew it he was flying through the air.

'Dratted cat!' the captain roared. 'Yowling like a sea-witch in my ear! The bird never does that!'

4.

Scratch to the Rescue

Scratch landed on his feet and then skidded on the sloping deck. He was almost trodden on by Flop-eye Fred, who was looking for Squawk.

'Ahoy, there, Flop-eye!' yelled the captain. 'Get a move on, you jellyfish!'

Scratch ducked behind a pile of torn sails which lay on the foredeck.

Fred was searching through heaps of canvas, inside piles of rope and under the parrot's cage.

'Where's that useless bird?' Captain Patch roared. 'Kate will never talk to me again if I come home without it!'

Scratch looked up to see if Squawk was still being a seagull. He could hear the gulls but all he could see was flapping sails.

So he crept out of his hiding place
and scrambled up the rigging to the
first yardarm. When his view was
still blocked by sails and ropes, he
clawed higher.

At last Scratch saw the parrot.
He wasn't being a seagull any more.
He was more like a flag. A ragged
black pirate pennant fluttered from
the very top of the main mast,
and Squawk was clinging to the
end of it.

'Help me, Splash!' the parrot
screeched.

Down below, the captain was
still roaring for his bird. Scratch
scrambled higher, gripping with all
his claws.

At last he was clinging to the very tip of the mast. Seagulls wheeled around him. Squawk flapped at the end of the pennant. Below them, the sails billowed and bulged, and below that was the deep blue sea.

Scratch reached out and hooked the pennant with a claw. Then, claw by claw, he reeled the parrot towards him.

'I can't fly any more,' whimpered the parrot. 'My wings are too sore.'

'Then I'll have to carry you in my mouth,' said Scratch.

The parrot closed his eyes. 'Please don't bite!' he whispered.

With his mouth full of feathers, Scratch began the long climb back down. It was harder than climbing up. It soon felt as if his claws were ripping out. Then it felt as if his paws were coming off. It wasn't long before long he lost his grip and fell.

He landed at Spike's feet.

'The cat's caught a rat!' Spike shouted. 'No, it's a seagull. No, it's the parrot!'

Flop-eye and Stinky came running. They had to rescue the parrot before the captain saw what had happened. But Scratch got up and ran straight to the bridge, followed by a crowd of horrified pirates.

Scratch laid the parrot at the captain's feet. 'I found your bird!' he yowled.

'What in the blazes . . .!' roared the captain.

Squawk lay still and bedraggled on the deck. Scratch gave him a gentle nudge with his nose.

'If that bird's dead,' Curly Joe muttered, 'we're all in trouble.'

Scratch nudged again. 'Come on, bird!' he mewed. 'Wake up!'

Squawk suddenly opened his eyes.

'Shiver me fingers!' he squawked, scrambling to his feet.

Then he fluttered his wings and flapped unsteadily up to Captain Patch's shoulder.

'*Awk*! Pieces of Kate!' he shrieked. 'Scraps the cat! Splash the cat! Sharrk!'

'That cat was trying to eat the bird!' roared the captain. 'First the mice, and now the parrot. You all know what happens to anyone who threatens my Kate's parrot!'

The crew didn't like it when the captain was in a bad mood. Anything could happen, and they didn't want it to happen to them. The best thing to do was make sure it happened to someone else.

'Blow me down, Cap'n!' said Bad Benji. 'I think you're right!'

'What a bad cat!' cried Curly Joe.

Flop-eye and Stinky made a grab at Scratch. Scratch swiped at their hairy hands with his magnificent claws and darted away. He ran to the rear deck and dived under a bundle of filthy rags.

He stayed there for the rest of the day.

Late that night Scratch sneaked out and went to visit Squawk. The bird drooped on his perch. He was tired and sore from all the flying he had done. His wings flopped and his head hung down.

'Scraps, you were wrong,' he croaked. 'I'm not cut out to be a freegull. They laughed at me and called me a feather duster!'

'Never mind,' said Scratch. 'We'll find another way to give you a peaceful life. We just have to work out what your real talents are.'

They didn't have time to work out what those talents were. Just then Spike came along and took Squawk out of his cage, and Scratch had to make a run for it.

'Off to see the captain,' said Spike. 'You've got a job to do, bird, just like the rest of us.'

5.
A Special Kind of Carrot

Scratch spent the rest of the night crouched behind a pile of sails. He kept dreaming about walking the plank, so he tried to stay awake and think happy thoughts. He remembered the days in the galley on the *Silk'n'Spice*, watching Peg-leg chop onions, potatoes and carrots for his famous stews.

This gave Scratch an idea. It was a silly idea, but the parrot was a silly bird. He scratched under his chin to clear his mind, then set off in the early dawn to visit Squawk.

The parrot was back in his cage, as sad and drooping as ever.

'Woe is me,' said Squawk. 'I had to sit on the captain's shoulder all evening while he smoked a cigar and sang shanties. It's no life for me.'

'Cheer up,' said Scratch. 'I've worked out how to help you.'

'*Awwwk*! Not a freegull again!' squeaked Squawk. 'You were very kind to help me, but look what happened last time!'

'It's another idea,' said Scratch.

'I don't know,' sighed Squawk.
'It all seems too hard.'

'I think the captain might be hard
of hearing,' Scratch said.

'Tardy steering? That's Benji's job!'

'Hard of hearing. Deaf. When Kate
said you were a ship's parrot, I think
she really meant ship's *carrot*.'

Squawk's beak fell open. 'You
mean ... I'm not really a parrot?
I'm a carrot?'

Scratch looked closely at Squawk.
Would he really believe it?

'Yes!' he mewed. 'You aren't
supposed to sit on a pirate's shoulder
at all!'

'*Aarrk*! Red man's chest and walk the tank!' Squawk flapped his wings happily. Then he stopped. 'There's just one thing. What's a carrot?'

'Well, a carrot is like ... er ... treasure. Pirates collect carrots and ... er ... put them in baskets. You'd love the peaceful life of a ship's carrot, Squawk. I've seen carrots sleep in a snug basket for days and days.'

'But what is a carrot's job?' asked Squawk. 'The captain likes everyone to have a job.'

Scratch had to think about that for a bit.

'Just to lie around and look beautiful,' he said at last. 'The other carrots on this ship are plain orange.

But you're blue, and green, and yellow, and red. You'd be the most beautiful carrot of all.'

Squawk preened. 'Yes, I *am* lovely! Maybe you should show me this carrot basket. I need a bit of a rest after my adventures.'

Scratch set off for the storeroom with the parrot perched on his shoulder. He stayed in the shadows so no one would see them slip down a hatch to the food-store.

'Now, Squawk, this is the . . . er . . . treasure store. Here is the carrot basket, and here are the other carrots. See how peaceful they are!'

Squawk hopped onto the rim of the basket. 'What do I do now?'

The parrot was so silly that Scratch had to show him. He jumped into the basket and lay still and straight and stiff among the carrots. By the time Squawk was lying in the basket, Scratch was sick and tired of being a carrot. But Squawk was very happy.

Then Scratch padded off to find the captain. He would find a way to get onto the pirate's shoulder, and this time he would stay there.

6.
Scratch to the Rescue—Again!

Scratch stood in the doorway of the captain's cabin and peered in. The bed was unmade and the captain's nightclothes lay crumpled in the dust and mouse droppings on the floor. Captain Patch was sitting at a wobbly desk, writing a letter. Scratch crept noiselessly across the cabin and crouched under the captain's chair.

The captain sounded out the words aloud as he wrote.

'Dearest Kate,' he said. 'I wish you were here. The parrot is well. We have many days of sailing ahead. We picked up a ship's cook and a cat. The cook might be worth lots of gold but I don't know about the cat. It caught a mouse and tried to kill the parrot. It'll go overboard next time.

From your loving Ivan.'

Scratch dived under the bed and stayed there, too scared to move. How would he be able to sit on the captain's shoulder if the captain didn't trust him?

When he had finished the letter, Captain Patch took out his bag of gold coins and started counting. When he counted them a second time he got a different amount. The next time was different again. He kept counting all afternoon.

At last the captain's belly gave an enormous rumble. 'Shiver me timbers,' he grumbled. 'I could eat a whale!'

He stretched, scratched his belly, and strolled out the door.

Scratch slunk from under the bed and slid out after him. He followed the captain on silent paws, waiting for a chance to escape up onto the deck. Captain Patch headed for the bridge with his spyglass, and Scratch visited the galley to see if Peg-leg would throw him a scrap of food.

Peg-leg was running late with the dinner. There was a mound of potatoes and a basket of vegetables still waiting to be chopped. He had been cutting up onions and was wiping his eyes with his beard.

Scratch thought he would wait until Peg-leg's eyes stopped watering. But suddenly there were footsteps and Captain Patch loomed in

the doorway. Scratch slid behind a
flour cask.

'Where's our grub?' the captain
roared. 'The men are hungry!
Why can't I smell any cooking?'

Peg-leg began chopping madly.
'It's almost ready, sir,' he sniffled.
'Potato and onion soup with turnips
and fresh carrots! Any minute now!'

'Get on with it and stop snivelling!'
Captain Patch grunted. Then he
shouted. 'You, Spike! Fetch the
parrot!'

Spike dashed away, and the captain
went to peer through his spyglass on
the lookout for treasure islands.

Scratch's fur bristled with horror.
When Peg-leg mentioned carrots,
Scratch had a horrible thought.
He crept from behind the cask and
looked up at the bench. There were
fresh carrots up there, all right! One
of the carrots was so fresh it was still
breathing—a breathing, feathery,
multicoloured carrot! Peg-leg was
snatching vegetables from the basket
and chopping like crazy.

When Peg-leg turned to dump
some onions into the pot, Scratch
leapt quickly onto the bench.

'Look out, Squawk!' he hissed.

Squawk kept his eyes shut.

'Go away, Scratch. I'm enjoying this.
I haven't had such fun since . . .'

Scratch batted him with his paw.
'Wake up, Squawk! Peg-leg is about
to put you in the dinner!'

The parrot opened one eye.
'I'm thinner?'

'You're dinner! You must escape
before you get chopped up!'

'Chopped!' screeched Squawk.
'Help! Help!'

He fluttered his wings. And then he fainted.

Peg-leg turned back to the bench. At the same moment Captain Patch came back to check on dinner. They both saw Scratch standing among the vegetables, licking the parrot.

Squawk shivered and woke up. 'Scraps! *Awwk!*' he squeaked.

'Look at that, Captain! The cat's gone and . . . and got your bird again!' said Peg-leg.

Captain Patch stretched to his full height and bumped his head on the ceiling. 'Blister my barnacles!' he cried. 'What's the bird doing beside your cooking pot, man! And the cat at it again! What will Kate say?'

He picked up the parrot and placed it on his shoulder. Squawk hooked his claws into the captain's curly black beard and fainted again.

Captain Patch shook a fist at Scratch.

'Watch out, you scurvy little furball. I'll be watching you closely! If it weren't for Kate's soft heart, I'd do something very painful to you!'

That night, Scratch did not sleep for a long time. He had too much thinking to do. His main thought was that perhaps he should worry more about Squawk and less about himself. He was no closer to the captain's shoulder, but Squawk had nearly died twice. It didn't seem right. But by the time his tail was perfectly clean with not a hair out of place, he had the glimmer of a new idea . . .

7.
The Best Friend
Is a Happy Friend

Scratch sat beside the parrot's cage
the following morning.

'I would have been the next carrot
in the pot,' said Squawk, 'if it wasn't
for you. You are the best friend a bird
could have.'

Scratch licked a foot. He didn't
want to say it was his fault the parrot
had been a carrot in the first place.

'Sailors are a careless lot,' he said.
'But you're safe now.'

'Safe, but unhappy, Scraps. I just want to sit here in my cage, but in a few minutes I'll have to go and sit on the captain's shoulder again.'

'I've been thinking,' said Scratch.

'Again?' said Squawk.

'I just want you to be happy,' said Scratch. 'And the happiest bird I ever saw was a pigeon. He had made a snug nest in a safe hole and he just sat there cooing, waiting for a girl pigeon to put eggs in it.'

Squawk's eyes shone and he sat straighter on his perch.

'There are many places on a pirate ship for snug nests,' Scratch went on.

'And plenty of rubbish lying around
to build the nest from.'

After getting Scratch to explain
seven times what a parrot could use
for a nest, and where snug holes
might be found, the bird flew off.
Scratch watched him go, then
padded to a safe hiding spot on
the poop deck to keep an eye on
Captain Patch.

It wasn't long before there was a roar. '*Aaaargghh*!! My beard!' yelled the captain. 'What are you doing, you dratted bird?'

Only Scratch knew that Squawk was gathering hair from the captain's beard to line his nest with.

A little later Peg-leg shouted some rude words from the galley where Squawk had stolen straw from the egg basket and broken six eggs. Then Benji yelled even ruder words when Squawk pulled some loose threads from the Jolly Roger. The nest was going well.

Meanwhile, every morning, Squawk sat in his cage looking as sad and sick as he could.

And every morning, when Captain Patch saw him, he said, 'That bird looks unwell. He'd best stay in his cage.'

Once the coast was clear, Squawk left the cage and flew to his nest in the snug hole he'd found inside the barrel of the big cannon on the foredeck. It was a lovely spot with a view of the waves, just in front of the cannonball. Squawk sat there all day, watching the sea and waiting for a mate to come by. He was happy. He was peaceful. And he didn't have to be a pirate's parrot.

Meanwhile, Scratch no longer wanted the parrot's job. It was too dangerous.

Scratch just wanted Squawk to
be happy. And he wanted to get
home safe. The best way to do that,
he thought, was to stay hidden.
So that's what he did.

8.
Attack!

Flop-eye Fred and Toothless Terry stared gloomily at the horizon. They hadn't raided a single ship or found a single treasure island since their trip began. If they didn't find something soon, they would go home with nothing.

Scratch crouched above them on the first yardarm.

'I've searched the horizon again and again,' grumbled Flop-eye, 'but all I can see is grey clouds.'

'Looks like a storm blowing up,' said Toothless.

The light was growing dimmer and the clouds were soon overhead. A strong wind started rattling the sails.

'We'd better tell the captain,' said Flop-eye.

'You tell him,' said Toothless.

'Flipping weather,' said Flop-eye. 'Now it's raining.'

'I'll stay here and watch for rocks,' said Toothless. 'You go and tell the captain.'

'You're always telling me what to do,' said Flop-eye. 'You do it!'

He gave Toothless a push. Toothless
shoved him back. Flop-eye tripped
and fell. He grabbed Toothless's leg
and pulled him down. They rolled
about on the deck, slapping and
kicking and shouting.

Meanwhile the captain had
already noticed there was a storm
brewing.

'Get yourselves moving,' he bellowed, marching around on deck. 'Trim the sails and tie down the gear!'

Pirates swarmed up the rigging and across the decks as the ship began to lurch on the growing waves.

Suddenly Flop-eye put his hand to his head. '*Owww*!'

Then Toothless shouted '*Owww*!' and held his head too.

They glared at each other as the thunder rumbled. Loud thumps hit the decks around them.

'Enemy fire!' screamed Toothless. 'We're under attack!'

The pirates stopped tying down gear, raced to the rail and peered out to sea.

'It's not enemy fire!' Spike yelled. 'It's just—'

'Shut up, cabin boy!' growled Benji. 'This is pirate work, so what would you know?'

Captain Patch came from the bridge with his spyglass. 'Attack?' he roared. 'We'll see about that. Fire the big gun!'

Scratch bristled in horror and scrambled down the rigging. 'You mustn't fire that gun!' he yowled.

He bounded across the deck and leapt to the ship's rail, close to the gunport. He howled and waved his tail.

The pirates took no notice.

They were too busy looking for the
attacking ship out in the heaving sea.

Spike tapped the captain's arm.
'Sir, it's only—' he began.

Captain Patch elbowed him away.

Scratch clung to the flaking
wooden rail as the ship heaved up
one side of a surging wave and
plunged down the other side.

Ker-thud! A heavy object landed on the deck, and smashed to pieces. It was followed by another.

'Fire!' roared Captain Patch.

'But, Captain!' shouted Spike.

Benji knocked Spike to the deck.

9.

The Valiant Cat

Fred lit the fuse and the cannon boomed. The cannonball burst out with a roar. In front of it flew a little basket made of black hair, canvas threads, seagull feathers and straw. Perched inside the basket was a startled parrot. The cannonball forged ahead into the darkness as the nest dropped gently to the water.

A flash of orange, green, red, yellow
and blue caught Captain Patch's eye.
'What was that?' he shouted and
raised his spyglass. 'Where did it go?'

The pirates pushed and shoved,
yelling as they reloaded the cannon.
Bang! Another ball flew into the
darkness. The explosion lit up the
water.

'There! Look, there!' yelled
Captain Patch.

For a moment a basket bobbed
into view on the pitching waves.

'Squawk! It's Squawk! Oh no!
What'll Kate say!'

Scratch didn't care what Kate
would say. He only cared about the
parrot. Without another thought
he launched himself into the dark,
heaving sea.

'*Yowwwrr*! Hold on, Squawk!'

Scratch struggled through the
enormous waves. He flattened his
ears and clamped his jaws to keep
the water out. Every now and then
he spotted the nest, only to lose
sight of it again.

By the time he reached the bird, the nest had fallen to pieces.

'No one will share it with me now!' croaked Squawk. 'You didn't tell me it had to be waterproof!'

'Never mind your nest!' Scratch spluttered. 'Fly back to the ship!'

'But I can't fly with wet feathers.'

'Then hop onto my head!'

The parrot scrambled onto Scratch's head and dug his claws firmly into the kitten's skull.

'Do we fire again, Captain?' shouted Benji.

'There's no need!' squeaked Spike.

But Captain Patch had forgotten all about the cannon.

'Look at that cat!' he shouted, pointing out at the heaving swell.

The pirates clung to the rail and stared. There was Scratch, swimming as hard as he could with the bird clinging to his head.

'*Aaark*!' screeched the parrot. 'Shaaarrk!'

'Throw him a rope, you lubbers!' yelled Captain Patch.

In no time twenty ropes dangled overboard.

Scratch locked his claws into the nearest one and hung on as he and Squawk were hauled up the side of the ship. Safe at last, Scratch crouched on the deck, coughing and shivering. His ginger fur lay wet and dark and sleek against his skin. Squawk still clung to his head.

Captain Patch swooped on them and prised the parrot's claws out of Scratch's skull. 'What were you doing in the cannon, you idiot bird?' he asked.

Scratch cowered and shivered some
more. Any minute now the captain
would make him walk the plank.

'But, Captain!' cried Toothless.
'What about the enemy attack?'

'It was hail,' yelled Spike. 'Not
enemy fire!'

'He's right,' said Benji. 'Look. Hailstones!'

The hail hammered down and the pirates scuttled to batten the hatches.

Captain Patch stowed the parrot inside his jacket. Then he picked up Scratch. 'Saving the bird has saved my life, too, Valiant Cat,' he said. 'I don't know what Kate would have done to me if I'd lost the bird at sea.'

He wiped the salt water out of
Scratch's eyes and then he put him on
his shoulder. Scratch dug in his claws
and held on tight.

But the only sound he made was a
salty purr.

How It All Ended

The *Patch's Glory* sailed into port
on a wet and windy day. Twenty
scruffy sailors rushed down the
gangplank, followed by Bad Benji
and Peg-leg. Peg-leg was staying
on as ship's cook on the *Patch's Glory*.
He and Benji were going to shop
for provisions for the captain's
honeymoon cruise.

Last of all came Captain Patch.
On his shoulder sat a plump ginger
kitten with a very fine tail. In the
captain's hand was a cage with a
cheerful parrot safely inside.

'Pieces of Kate!' it screeched. 'Polly
wants a smacker!'

Captain Patch headed straight for
a young woman waiting on the quay.

She wore a frilly pink dress with a frilly pink hat, and was carrying a frilly pink parasol and frilly pink handbag.

'Ivan, darling!' the woman cried. 'How well Squawk looks!'

She threw her arms around Captain Patch. Her golden curls bounced like springs as she laid her head on his shoulder. Scratch sniffed at a bobbing curl and sneezed.

Kate jumped backwards. 'A *cat!*' she screeched.

Scratch arched his back and hissed.

'Cats don't belong on *my* darling's shoulder!' Kate hissed back. She swung her pink parasol at Scratch.

He ducked and the parasol hit the
captain on the side of his head.

Scratch swished his tail and spat.
Kate threw her frilly pink bag at him.
Scratch dug in his claws and yowled.
The bag hit Patch on the nose.

'Hang on a minute, Kate!' he
snuffled. 'This cat saved Squawk's life!'

'I don't care what it did. It can't have your shoulder. Your shoulder is for a pirate's parrot or for my golden curls. Get off, you fluffy fleabag!'

'But I promised the cat a life of luxury!' croaked Captain Patch.

'Not likely!' she answered. The parasol swung again.

Scratch jumped off Captain Patch's shoulder onto a stack of barrels. He didn't know where he was going, but anything was better than being beaten with a frilly pink parasol.

Captain Patch gazed into Kate's eyes. He had already forgotten Scratch. But as Scratch sat to wash his shoulder, he heard a parrot voice.

'Yo ho ho and a scratch on the tum,
Wash behind the ear and a lick on
the bum.
Scraps is the friend I hold most dear,
So stroke his head and tickle his rear!
Awwwwk!'

Scratch would miss his feathery friend. He gave a little purr, then jumped down from the barrels. It was time to look for another ship. One that needed a brave ship's kitten.

Words Sailors Use

batten the hatches	to fasten the hatches so they don't fly open in a storm or battle
bridge	a raised platform from where the sailor in charge navigates the ship
crow's nest	a small basket at the top of mast where a sailor could sit and look out for approaching land or danger
cutlass	a short, heavy, curved sword used by pirates and other sailors
fore-and-aft	the front ("fore") and back ("aft") of a ship
foredeck	the deck at the front of a ship
galley	a ship's kitchen
gangplank	a plank used as a temporary bridge for getting on or off a ship
gunport	a hole in the side of a ship through which the cannons are fired
hatch	an opening in the ship's deck, covered by a watertight lid
helm	the steering wheel on a sailing ship
Jolly Roger	the pirate flag, showing a white skull and crossbones on a black background
landlubber	somebody who has never been to sea
lubber	a clumsy sailor
mainsail	the most important sail on a sailing ship, raised from the main mast

mast	a stout pole rising straight up from the deck of a ship, which supports the yards and sails
pennant	a triangular flag
poop deck	the roof of the poop cabin, which is found at the back of a ship
prow	the front part of a ship which is above the waterline
quay	a place for ships to unload or load their cargoes
rigging	the ropes and chains used to support and move the sails
scurvy	an illness. Olden-day sailors often suffered from scurvy on long voyages because they could not store fresh food. To call another sailor "scurvy" was an insult.
shanty/shanties	a sailors' song
shipshape	in good order, tidy and well-arranged
spyglass	a small telescope
trim the sails	to adjust the sails
walk the plank	to make a person walk along a plank stuck out over the side of a ship until they fall off the end, into the sea
yardarm	either end of a yard of a square sail. A "yard" is the name given to the wooden post attached cross-ways to the mast, from which the sail is hung.

About the Author

Jessica Green has always loved cats, and shares her home with four furry feline friends— Fang, Felis, Tre and Tumnus. She has never had a cat quite like Scratch, but she once had a mad little three-legged cat called Gilbert who used to get into all kinds of strife.

Jessica learned a lot about life at sea when she tried sailing with her husband in his yacht. She soon realised that she hated being cold and wet, falling overboard, and being shouted at!

About the Artist

Mitch Vane would love to run away to sea but she can't because after half an hour on a boat she gets seasick!

Mitch once had a cat called George. He was a lot like Scratch and liked to sit on the newspaper when Mitch was trying to read it!

Nowadays Mitch has a cat called Patchy. Mitch and her family love Patchy a lot, but not when she leaps up and down the hall at three in the morning.

Acknowledgements

Thanks to Michael, for trying, and failing,
to teach me to love the water.

Thanks to Nick, Richard and Gillian,
for assuring me that writing about mad
kittens is far more useful than a tidy house.

Thanks to Mitch, for seeing Scratch
so clearly.

Special thanks to Margrete, for planting the
idea of Scratch into my mind.

Jessica

For more exciting action with
the swashbuckling

SCRATCH KITTEN

look out for the third adventure . . .

SCRATCH KITTEN
and the
RAGGED REEF